To the Easter
Chicken's good
friend,
Adam —
Enjoy!!
Lisa Wille
2012

The Easter Chicken

Lisa Funari Willever
Lorraine Funari

Illustrated by Emma Overman

Special Guest Young Author & Illustrator Section

Franklin Mason Press
Trenton, New Jersey

To my son, Patrick Timothy...LFW

To my daughter, Lisa. Thank you for inviting me to share this
wonderful experience with you...LF

To my parents, who read me my first book...EO

The editors at Franklin Mason Press would like to offer their gratitude to those who have contributed their time, energy, and support to this project: Mrs. Rebecca Matthias, Mr. Clarence Vandegrift, Mrs. Suzanne Rhoads, Mrs. Lisa Battinelli, Ms. Geraldine Willever, Sr. Marie Anthony, Dr. Patricia Kempton, Ms. Wanda Bowman, Ms. Nancy Volpe, Ms. Dawn Hiltner, Ms. Stacey Williams, Mr. Robert Quackenbush, Ms. Patti Willever, Mr. Harold Wolf, Ms. Kim Koch and Mrs. Elizabeth H. Rossell along with our dear friends at the Princeton Chapter of S.C.O.R.E. (Service Corps of Retired Executives) and SPAN (Small Publishers Association of North America). Also, a special thanks to those who have worked on the Guest Young Author & Guest Young Illustrator Committees. Your care in selecting the work of young authors and artists will help to shape and inspire the writers and illustrators of tomorrow.

Published in the United States

Printed in Singapore

Franklin Mason Press ISBN No. 0-9679227-6-3

Library of Congress Control Number: 00-135787

10 9 8 7 6 5 4 3

St. Jude Children's
Research Hospital
ALSAC · Danny Thomas, Founder

Franklin Mason Press is proud to support the important work of
St. Jude Children's Research Hospital. In that spirit, $0.25 will be
donated from the sale of each book.

Thanksgiving was over and Christmas had passed,
but Easter, oh, Easter, was coming so fast.

With no turkey leftovers and Rudolph retired,
once again, once again, that Bunny was hired.

It's not fair, thought the chicken, each year it's the same.
He gets the best job, then he gets all the fame.

What is so special, what has he got?
What can he do, that a chicken cannot?

His tail may be fluffy and soft as can be,
but what makes him think that he's better than me?

I may have a hard beak, not a pink little nose
and my feet aren't cute, like his fur covered toes.

1 I have no floppy ears, and oh, I should mention . . .
no whiskers like his, that just stand at attention.
So I'm covered with feathers and have little legs,
I think I'm cute and I can lay eggs!

There's more to this chicken than warming the nest.
From my point of view, I'd be the BEST!

I would do all the work and I'd get the job done,
while that floppy'ear furball just plays in the sun.

He plays with the chipmunks, the beavers, the fawn and one day a year, he leaves eggs on the lawn.

Big deal, thought the chicken, to hop yard to yard. If a bunny can do it, it can't be too hard.

His days they are numbered and this much I know,
it's time for a chicken, THE BUNNY MUST GO!

This hard working chicken will get the job done,
I'll do all the work and I'll even have fun!

I'll lay all the eggs, from the small to the large,
I'll lay enough eggs to fill up a barge.
I'll boil the eggs while I whistle a tune,
I'll paint every egg and I'll be done by noon.

1

I'll take a long lunch, an hour or more.
I'll load up my basket, then go door to door.

For once I'll be famous and I'll get the credit.
I'll love my new job and I'll never regret it.

So down by the pond, where the bunny was swimming,
the chicken walked up and boy was she grinning.

"Let's make a deal, ol' bunny, ol' pal.
You have Easter each year, BUT I WANT IT NOW!"

The bunny looked up for a moment or two
and asked if the chicken had thought her plan through.

"I'm not sure, little chicken, you have what you'll need.
For delivering eggs requires great speed."

"Those short little legs may do well on the farms,
but how will you work with two wings and no arms?

You lay the best eggs that I ever did see,
so why don't you just leave delivering to me?"

"Go back to your carrots! Stay out of my way!
Easter is mine, now, starting today!"

Then she left for the kitchen, with so much to do . . .
cooking, then coloring, and delivering, too.

When the laying was done and the water was ready,
she carried the eggs, she carried them steady.
But before she could boil them, once and for all,
one by one, egg by egg, they started to fall.

As she boiled the rest, chicken whistled no tune
and she knew she would never be finished by noon.

She didn't give up, didn't moan, didn't whine.
She painted each egg with a different design.

She yawned every minute, at least once or twice
and she thought to herself, that a nap would be nice.

But the clock kept on ticking, she knew it was late
and the nap that she needed would just have to wait.

She loaded the basket and when she was done,
the basket she loaded, it weighed half a ton!
It was clear that she needed much more than good luck,
to move this big basket, she'd need a big truck!

After thinking it over, she knew what to do,
and she rushed to the pond, to find ol' you know who.
The bunny looked up with a sly little grin,
to think of the trouble the chicken was in.

"What's wrong little chicken, you don't look so cheery.
In fact, I would say that you look kind of weary."

"The truth is, bunny, it's time to confess,
Easter's in trouble. I've made a huge mess!"

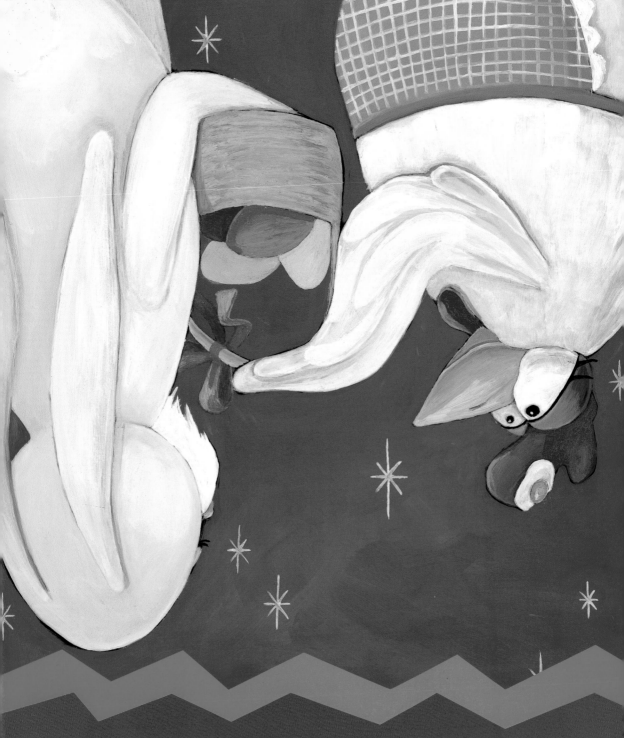

But the bunny just chuckled and said that he knew,
it was much, too much work for one chicken to do.

"What was I thinking? I should have known better.
To do a job right, we must all work together!"

A As the chicken went home for that much needed rest,
the bunny left eggs from the east to the west.
She hoped he had time, she hoped he would hurry,
but the bunny was fast, there was no need to worry.

She awoke the next morning, just before dawn,
to see dozens and dozens of eggs on each lawn.
Pink eggs, green eggs, yellow and blue.
Easter was saved 'cause the bunny came through!

But that wasn't all, there was one thing more,
a special surprise when she opened the door.

The End

A basket of goodies, filled end to end,
With love, from the Bunny. . .the chicken's new friend!

Guest Young Author

Matthew Rosidivito — Age 9
Franklin School
Trenton, New Jersey
"Dashing Through The Snow!"

It was a cold winter night and signs of Christmas were everywhere. Mom and I decided to go for a drive and see some lights and decorations. We drove to a town where all of the houses were brightly decorated. We were going very slowly when a row of cars came up behind us. Mom pulled to the side of the road to let the cars go by. We started to pull onto the road again. To our surprise, the van started sinking! At first, we thought it was our imagination, but I could see the dashboard slowly lean to the side. Soon, a pair of sunglasses slid down to the floor.

My mom got out and stepped into six inches of something very slushy. She tried to pull her foot out and her shoe came off! She tried her other foot and that shoe came off, too. I was scared and wanted to come out of the car. I put my foot down and it sank into the thick, black mud. I was stuck and as mom tried to pull me out, we both fell in! We looked up and saw a man and woman walking their dog. We tried to stand up so they could see us. They saw us stuck in the ditch and helped get our van out. Next, they directed us to a car wash where we jet sprayed the van with soap and hot water. At the same time, mom and I splashed ourselves clean. Together with the van, we were one gigantic soap sud. Later that night we returned home as if nothing had happened. It was a while before we told everyone about our funny adventure.

John Farelli — Age 8
Roosevelt School
River Edge, New Jersey

"The Apple Fell Far From the Tree
(and Landed On My Brother's Head!)"

Abdul Smith — Age 9
Joyce Kilmer School
Trenton, New Jersey

"My Magic Sneakers "

1st

TIE
Kyle Czepiel — Age 9
& Ryan Czepiel — Age 9
Antheil Elementary School
Ewing, New Jersey
"At The Jersey Shore"

1st

Kyle Czepiel

Ryan Czepiel

2nd

TIE
Lauren B. Davis — Age 7
Marian McKeown School
Newton, New Jersey
"The Chicken Hunt"

Ben LeBlanc
Age 8
Rayne, Louisiana
"We Love St. Jude's"

2nd

3rd

Taylor Oakley   Age 7
Immaculate Conception School
Trenton, New Jersey

"My Favorite Mermaid"

Would You Like To Be An Author or Illustrator?

Franklin Mason Press is looking for stories and illustrations from children ages 6-9 to appear in our books. We are dedicated to providing young authors and illustrators with an avenue into the world of publishing.

If you would like to be our next Guest Young Author or Guest Young Illustrator, read the information below and the rules on the next page.

To be a Guest Young Author :

Write a 75–200 word story about something that is strange, funny, or unusual.

To be a Guest Young Illustrator :

Draw a picture using crayons, markers or colored pencils.

Prizes

1st. Place Author / 1st. Place Illustrator

$25.00 and your work will be published in FMP's newest book.

2nd. Place Author / 2nd. Place Illustrator

$15.00 and your name will be published in FMP's newest book.

3rd. Place Author / 3rd. Place Illustrator

$10.00 and your name will be published in FMP's newest book.

Rules For The Contest

1. Children may enter one category only, either Author or Illustrator.

2. All stories must be typed.

3. All illustrations must be sent in between two pieces of cardboard to prevent wrinkling.

4. Name, address, phone number, age, school, and parent's signature must be on the back of all submissions.

5. All work must be original and completed solely by the child.

6. Franklin Mason Press reserves the right to print submitted material. All work becomes property of FMP and will not be returned. Any work selected is considered a work for hire and FMP will retain all rights.

7. There is no deadline for submissions. FMP will publish children's work in every book published. All submissions will be considered for the next available book.

8. All submissions should be sent to: Youth Submissions Editor, Franklin Mason Press, P.O. Box 3808, Trenton, NJ 08629—www.franklinmasonpress.com

Tips for Young Authors & Illustrators

1. Write and draw about things you enjoy. If you need an idea, think of your family, your friends, or your favorite things to do.

2. Find a nice quiet place where you can write or draw.

3. If you are having trouble beginning your story, make a list of ideas that you want to write about. Use your list to get started.

4. If you become stuck in the middle of a story, put it away and go back to it the next day. Sometimes all you will need is to take a break or get some rest.

5. Remember, your first draft of a story is never your last draft. Rewrite, rewrite, rewrite…until it's perfect.

6. Share your stories and illustrations with your family, friends, and teachers.

7. If you are between the ages of 6-9 years old, send your work to Franklin Mason Press…Home of the Guest Young Author and Illustrator Contest!

About Franklin Mason Press

Franklin Mason Press was founded in Trenton, New Jersey in September 1999. While our main goal is to produce quality reading materials, we also provide children with an avenue into the world of publishing. Our Guest Young Author and Illustrator Contest offers children an opportunity to submit their work and possibly become published authors and illustrators. In addition, Franklin Mason Press is proud to support children's charities with donations from book sales. Each new title benefits a different children's charity. For more information, please visit our website at:

www.franklinmasonpress.com

About St. Jude's Children's Research Hospital

St. Jude's Children's Research Hospital is the first institution established for the sole purpose of conducting basic and clinical research into catastrophic childhood diseases, mainly cancer. The hospital has approximately 4,000 patients in active status and treats children without regard to race, religion, creed or ability to pay. Fundraisers pay all costs of treatment not covered by insurance and families who have no insurance are never asked to pay.

Welcome to the St. Jude's Art Gallery!

Bunny & Tea Party — Jessica Turri

Basket with Eggs — Breanna Wilson

Baby Chick — Lacey Medlin

Bunny & Basket — Lacey Tyler

We love St. Jude — Ben LeBlanc

About the Authors & Illustrator

Lisa Funari Willever (author) is a lifelong resident of Trenton, New Jersey and a fourth grade teacher in the Trenton School District. She is a graduate of The College of New Jersey and a member of the New Jersey Education Association and the New Jersey Reading Association. The author of *The Culprit Was A Fly*, *Miracle On Theodore's Street*, and *Maximilian the Great*, this is her fourth children's picture book. Her husband, Todd, is a professional Firefighter in the city of Trenton and the co-author of *Miracle On Theodore's Street*, They are the proud parents of two year old, Jessica Marie and one year old, Patrick.

Lorraine Funari (author) a lifelong resident of Mercer County, New Jersey and the mother of three grown children, Lisa, Anthony, and Paula. Her husband, Reynold, is a meat cutter in Ewing, New Jersey. She is the co-author of *Maximilian the Great* and several upcoming titles.

Emma Overman (Illustrator) is a freelance illustrator and muralist. She received her Bachelor of Arts from Hanover College in Indiana and completed a Post Baccalaureate Program at Maryland Institute College of Art. Born in Brazil and raised in Tennessee, Emma now resides in Indianapolis, Indiana. This is her first children's book.

Franklin Mason Press

P.O. Box 3808, Trenton, NJ 08629
www.franklinmasonpress.com